Found.

JEFF NEWMAN & LARRY DAY

Simon & Schuster Books for Young Readers
New York London Toronto Sydney New Delhi

For Michele—J. N. · For Miriam—L. D.

SIMON & SCHUSTER BOOKS FOR YOUNG READERS
An imprint of Simon & Schuster Children's Publishing Division
1230 Avenue of the Americas, New York, New York 10020
Text copyright © 2018 by Jeff Newman · Illustrations copyright © 2018 by Larry Day
SIMON & SCHUSTER BOOKS FOR YOUNG READERS is a trademark of Simon & Schuster, Inc.
For information about special discounts for bulk purchases, please contact Simon & Schuster Special
Sales at 1-866-506-1949 or business@simonandschuster.com.
The Simon & Schuster Speakers Bureau can bring authors to your live event. For more information or to
book an event, contact the Simon & Schuster Speakers Bureau at 1-866-248-3049 or visit our website at
www.simonspeakers.com.
Book design by Lucy Ruth Cummins
The illustrations for this book were rendered in pen and ink with watercolor and gouache.
Manufactured in China · 0918 SCP · First Edition
2 4 6 8 10 9 7 5 3 1
Library of Congress Cataloging-in-Publication Data
Names: Newman, Jeff, 1976- author. | Day, Larry, 1956- illustrator.
Title: Found / Jeff Newman ; illustrated by Larry Day.
Description: First edition. | New York : Simon & Schuster Books for Young Readers, [2018] | Summary:
While Jenn is seeking Prudence, her big, sleek and shiny, black and white dog, she meets and falls in
love with Roscoe, a scruffy little golden dog.
Identifiers: LCCN 2017061219 (print) | LCCN 2018007872 (eBook) | ISBN 9781534410077 (eBook) |
ISBN 9781534410060 (hardcover)
Subjects: | CYAC: Lost and found possessions—Fiction. | Dogs—Fiction. | Stories without words.
Classification: LCC PZ7.N47984 (eBook) | LCC PZ7.N47984 Fo 2018 (print) | DDC [E]—dc23
LC record available at https://lccn.loc.gov/2017061219

Main Street
PET STORE